The Gingerbread Man

Illustrated by Elena Temporin

Retold by Mairi Mackinnon

Once upon a time, many years ago,

a little old woman

and a little old man
lived on a farm.

They were kind people.
It made them sad that they had no children.

"If only we had a little boy," sighed the old woman.

"I know!" she said one day. "I could make a boy out of gingerbread!"

So she took out her recipe book.
She weighed and she measured,

she mixed and
she stirred,

she rolled the dough
and she cut out a shape.

Then she put it in the oven to bake.

Soon the kitchen was filled with the smell of hot gingerbread.

"Almost ready now," said the old woman,
and opened the oven to look.

Mmmm

Out jumped a little gingerbread man!

He pattered across the kitchen floor...

...and ran right out of the open door!

"Stop!" called the old woman.

"Stop, stop!" called the old man.

But the gingerbread man
ran along the road, singing:

Run, run, as fast as you can,

You can't catch me

I'm the gingerbread man!

He raced past a horse
and a cow, grazing in the meadow.

"Mmm, you look delicious,"
neighed the horse.

"Come here, little man," mooed the cow.

But the gingerbread man ran along the road, singing:

I have run away from a little old woman and a little old man, and I can run away from you too, yes I can!

Run, run, as fast as you can,
You can't catch me
I'm the gingerbread man!

He sped past a farmer,
hard at work in a field.

"Mmm, what a treat,"
said the farmer.
"Come here, little man."

But the gingerbread man ran along the road, singing:

I have run away from a horse, a cow,

a little old woman and a little old man,

and I can run away from you too, yes I can!

Run, run, as fast as you can,

You can't catch me

I'm the gingerbread man!

He scampered past a school,

and all the children shouted,
"Mmm, we love gingerbread!
Come here, little man!"

But the gingerbread man ran along the road, singing:

I have run away from a farmer in a field, a horse, a cow,
a little old woman and a little old man,
and I can run away from you too, yes I can!

Run, run, as fast as you can,

You can't catch me

I'm the gingerbread man!

On and on he ran,
until he came to a river.

He wanted to cross it, but
he was afraid of getting wet.

A fox spotted him.
"If you climb onto my
tail, I'll help you across,"
he said.

The fox started swimming with the gingerbread man on his tail.

Soon, though, his tail was dragging in the water.

"I'm so sorry," said the fox.
"Do climb onto my back."

But soon the water was lapping over the fox's back.

"I'm so sorry," said the fox.
"Do climb onto my head."

The gingerbread man tiptoed
up to the fox's head...

The fox tossed his head, and SNAP!
The gingerbread man was a quarter gone.

SNAP! He was half gone.

SNAP! Three quarters gone...

SNAP! And that was the end of him.

Edited by Jenny Tyler and Lesley Sims
Designed by Louise Flutter
Cover design by Russell Punter